I0607025

Rober Craig Maclagan

**The Clan of the Bell of St. Fillan**

A Contribution to Gaelic Clan Etymology

Rober Craig Maclagan

**The Clan of the Bell of St. Fillan**
*A Contribution to Gaelic Clan Etymology*

ISBN/EAN: 9783743418707

Manufactured in Europe, USA, Canada, Australia, Japa

Cover: Foto ©Raphael Reischuk / pixelio.de

Manufactured and distributed by brebook publishing software
(www.brebook.com)

Rober Craig Maclagan

**The Clan of the Bell of St. Fillan**

# The Bell of St Fillan.

12 INCHES HIGH.

ANTIQUARIAN MUSEUM, EDINBURGH, 1879.

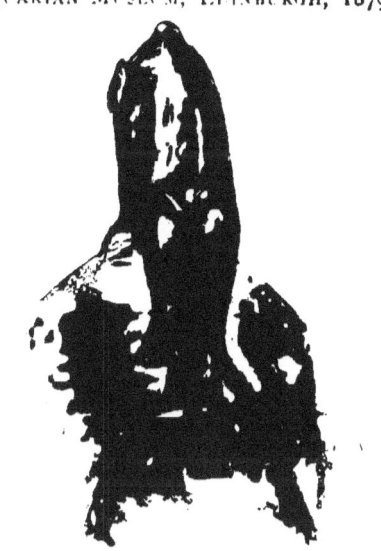

# Handle of Bell.

"'S DHEALAICH MISE RIU, 'S THUG EUD DHOMH, IM AIR EIBHLEIG, 'S BROCHAN
CAIL AN CREILEIG, 'S BROGA PAIPEIR, 'S CHUIR EUD AIR FOLBH MI LE PEI-
LEIR GUNNA-MHOIR 'AIR RATHAD-MOR GLOINE, GUS AN D'FHAG EUD A'M' SHUI-
DHE 'STAIGH AN SEO MI."

CAMPBELL'S TALES, *Ceabharnach*, Vol. I., p. 308.

*Literal translation*—" And I left them, and they gave me butter on a cinder, kail
porridge in a creel, and paper shoes; and they sent me away with a big gun
bullet, on a road of glass, till they left me here within "

THE

# CLAN OF THE BELL OF ST. FILLAN.

## 𝕬 Contribution to 𝕲aelic 𝕮lan 𝕰tymology.

BY

## ROBERT CRAIG MACLAGAN, M.D.,

### F.R.S.E., F.S.A. Scot.

———✦———

LIA, LIAE, *s.*, a great stone.

LIA-FÁIL, the Stone of Destiny, on which the ancient Irish monarchs used to be crowned until the time of Mortogh Mac Earc, who sent it into Scotland, that his brother Fergus, who had subdued that country, might be crowned on it. It is now in Westminster Abbey.—*Irish Gaelic Dictionary.*

LIA, *s. fem.*, a stone, a great stone.

LIA-FÀIL, E, *s. fem.* (Lia and Fàil, supposed Fàidheil), the stone on which the Scottish kings, and as some Irish writers say, the Irish kings, used to be crowned, and which is now in Westminster Abbey.—*Scottish Gaelic Dictionary.*

———✦———

*PRINTED FOR PRIVATE CIRCULATION.*

EDINBURGH:
PRINTED BY LORIMER AND GILLIES,
31 ST. ANDREW SQUARE.

# THE CLAN OF THE BELL OF ST. FILLAN.

———◆———

THAT a clan of Maclagans had their habitat near Logierait, called by the Gaelic-speaking inhabitants of Perthshire Laggan, may be regarded as indubitable from the frequency with which the clan name is met with thereabouts; and by an examination of the parish registers for a few years after the date of their commencement, from 1641 to 1762, the following facts have been obtained.

There were, during that time, 27 families resident in Logierait, 29 in Moulin, 19 in Dull, 20 in Scone, 17 in Dunkeld and Little Dunkeld, 5 in Perth, and the remainder of a total of about 148 in neighbouring parishes.

In the "Archæologia Scotica," vol. iv. p. 130, in a paper by the late Mr. Donald Gregory, it is said that in 1592 Archibald, Earl of Argyle, had a commission from the King and Council to raise the lieges against the M'Gregors in twenty-one parishes,— viz., Fortingal, Maclagan, Inchadin, Ardewnay, Killin, Strathfillan, &c. This would lead one to suppose that the parish called Maclagan lay to the west of Fortingal. On the south side of Loch Tay, near a place marked in the maps called Achomer, is a locality called Claggan to this day.

The Maclagan country thus seems well enough defined as being in the valleys of Tay and Tummel, but the irregularity of the registers, and the absence therefrom of several Maclagan families which are known to have existed there, leave us uninformed as to their numbers. Mr. Walter M'Leod, who made for me the searches, considers them to be numerically a third-rate clan.

The spelling of the name varies in two marked respects. Of

655 entries, 545 are spelt MacLagan, while 94 are spelt MacClagan
or MacKlagan, slight variations being introduced,—*e.g.*, *gg* in 69
instances, while an *e* is put at the end many times, and an *i* sometimes replaces the *a* of the last syllable; thus, Maclagine. The
earliest indisputable notice of them occurs in the " Book of Bands
of the Black Book of Taymouth," p. 200 :—

" Clan Teir [M'Intyre] give manrent to Sir Colin Campbell for the
slaughter of his foster-brother, Johne M'Gillenlag, 4 June, 1556, at
Glenurquhay. John Roy M'Ynteir deliverit to be punesit at the will of
the said Sir Colyne."*

In 1573 Duncan M'Lagan (so spelt in the Fasti) is presented to
the vicarage of Dull. He is called Maclaggane, and the date of
his appointment is 1561 in the " New Statistical Account." Again
in 1590 John Makclagene was translated from Kirk Michael to
Inchechaddin, the modern Kenmore.

In the household books of the " Black Book of Taymouth " at
Finlarig, beginning on Sunday, 26th August, 1621, to 2nd September, the guests are—" The Constable of Dundie and 2 sons tua
nichts, the young Laird tua nichts, Laird of Glenlyone tua nichts,
Robert of Glenfalloch, &c., tua nichts, the Laird of Macfarlane,
&c., tua nichts, the Barone of Argatie, ane nicht, Johne M'Clagan
& M'Neil tua nichts, wark folks, &c."

Inquiry in the Lyon Office yielded but small result. In a collection of blazons made by Joseph Stacie, a herald who died in
1687, not, however, as part of his original MS., but as a later
addition by a different hand, is the following entry :—

" M'lagan a branch of the M'Cleland. Or, two cheverons sable
within a bordure of the last. Crest, a Morter peice. Motto, Superba
Frango."

A herald named Martyn left an MS. of blazons collected about
a hundred years ago, and of no great value. He gives M'Lagan
the same arms, crest, and motto, except making the bordure gules.

In the following list of clans attached to the MacDougalls, the
MacLagans are included, which accords with a common tradition
that they are connected with that clan :—

---

* Possibly the M'Intyres of Glencoe in Glenurchie, said to be Macdonalds.
William Buchanan of Auchmar's essay " Of Clans."

" List of the different Clans and Tribes descended from the Family of Lorne, and of those depending on that most antient family, as kept in the Records thereof, viz. :

REALL MACDOUGALLS.

The MacDougalls of Lorn.
The MacIlvrides.
The MacIlechonils or Roys.
The MacEwens of Achomer, Perth, and Dungarthill.
The MacLagans.
The MacKeiths.
The MacPhersons in Moydart.
The MacNamuls in Jura.
The MacKellas in Barra.
The MacCillichans in Tyree.
The MacIllichears in Kintyre.
The Peddies in Perthshire.
The MacIllivartin Roys in Lochaber.
The MacVuldonich Dows in Glengarie.
The MacVeans and MacBeans of Lochaber and Perthshire.
The MacChruims.
The MacToincheirs.

DEPENDANTS.

The MacLulichs.
The MacLeas, improperly calling themselves Livingstones.
The MacInishes ⎫
The MacLellans ⎬ All MacInishes.
The MacVollans ⎪
The MacLucas's ⎭
The MacKeichans.
The MacIllichoans.
The MacCoans.
The MacIllivernochs, improperly calling themselves Grahams.
The MacInturnors or Turnors.
The MacKeigs.
The MacPheterishes.
The MacQueebans.
The MacAviaichs, improperly calling themselves M'Neils.
The MacCallums of Colgine.
The MacNaLearans, improperly calling themselves M'Leans.
The MacIntyres, many of them MacDougalls.
The MacIlevories.

" *N.B.*—The whole of the above tribes joined under MacDougall of Lorn's Banner or Double Colours, when he would have occasion to bring it to the ffield of strife and of honour. A true copy.

" EWEN MACDOUGALL."

Mr. John Sinclair MacLagan, of Glenquoich, from whom I received this list, says that at the date 1808, on the back of his copy, the Ewen who testifies to this was a schoolmaster at or near Aberfeldy, and a little of the *bon-vivant*.

I am indebted to Dr. MacLagan Wedderburn for the following :—

" The tradition as to the origin of our family [Dr. M'L. W. says he believes that to include all the Athole MacLagans], as I have heard it from my aunt, is as follows :—The three brothers who pursued Robert Bruce were of the clan of MacDougall of Lorn. Two, I believe, were killed, and Bruce left his cloak with the famous brooch in the hands of the third. The chief of the MacDougalls not only claimed the brooch, but wished to claim the honour of having taken it, and the survivor, afraid of being got rid of as an inconvenient witness of the truth, fled to Perthshire, where he took refuge either with the Earl of Athole or the Campbells, I forget which, and took the name of MacLagan. The only other tradition I remember, was as to the origin of the name, which she said was from the river Lagan in the north of Ireland. On some cattle-lifting expedition, a man swam across the river when in flood to recover a calf, and swam back with it; in remembrance of which feat his companions dubbed him the son of the Lagan. This man, however, had nothing to do with our family, who were really MacDougalls, and only adopted the name."

This tradition of the MacDougall connexion, and also the story of the swim in the north of Ireland, were known to members of my own family.

On the coat of arms used by my grandfather, Dr. David Maclagan, in addition to the chevrons of the M'Clellans, as quoted above, are three martlets, the " temple-haunting martlet " of Macbeth.

Thus the oldest derivation of the name, and the only semi-authoritative one, points to a connexion with the Galloway family of the M'Clellands (*Celtice*, Mac Gille Fhaelan, the "son of the servant of Fillan"), while the Maclagans are purely Perthshire;

and it seemed to me likely that the connecting link was to be looked for in the history of the " Fillans," two saints of that name being mentioned in the Scottish Calendars.

The first of these is described as—Faolan *anlobhar* of Rath Erann in Albain; and of Cill Fhaelain in Laoighis, in Leinster, of the race of Aenghus, son of Nadfraech, *i.e.*, King of Munster.*

The Gaelic epithet is capable of being translated either as composed of the definite article *am* prefixed to the noun *lobhar*, a leper; or of the prefix *an*, having a negative signification, and *labhair*, " speaking," *i.e.*, speaking with difficulty. According to these two etymologies, this Fillan is either Fillan the Leper, or Fillan the Stammerer.

Rath Erann is Dundurn, at the east end of Loch Earn, Perthshire; the Irish site, Kill Fhaelain, is in the parish of Kilcomanbane, in Queen's County.

This Fillan was a disciple of St. Ailbe, of Imluich (Emly, in Tipperary), Bishop of Munster, who, Tirechan says, was ordained a priest by St. Patrick. Ailbe died A.D. 541, St. Patrick in 493.

The second Fillan, to whom has been generally assigned the staff and bell in the Antiquarian Museum at Edinburgh, is said to have been "son of Feradach, probably of the race of Fiatach Finn " (a conjecture of which I have not been able to get an explanation), by Kentigerna, daughter of Cellach Cualan, King of Leinster. He received the habit and rule of his order from St. Mundus of Kilmun, whom he succeeded as abbot, and then seems to have gone to Glendeochquy to associate himself with St. Congan.

This Glendeochquy being doubtless the modern Glendochart, the two Fillans, assuming that there really were two individuals as above described, becoming located in the same district, were readily confounded one with the other. Such being the case, it is of little moment to which of the two the Fillan's churches at Loch Alsh, in Wigton, and in Renfrew, and the cave at Pittenweem are dedicated; but it is noteworthy that, while these churches and the cave were so called, what is held to have been their principal shrine bore a different name, Killin.

* " Martyr. Donegal," p. 175.

In Forbes' "Calendars," p. 463, he says of the name Wynnin :—

"That the language of the inhabitants of the Cymric kingdom of Strathclyde should be similar to that spoken in Wales proper, is only natural ; and if the Wynninus of Cuningham be the same as Finan, as Capgrave asserts, we have an instance of that softening of consonants which distinguishes the Welsh from the other forms of the Celtic. Wynnin is a local corruption of Gwynnin, Gw or Gu being the Welsh equivalent of the Irish Fai " (pronounced like *fay*, a fairy).

Here we have Finn and Gwynn identified, and I think this may be safely accepted as certain, and *Kill*, the church, *Fhinn*, of Finn, would become Killinn, the *fh* not being pronounced in Gaelic.

St. Patrick, who ordained Ailbe, the instructor of the first Fillan, had a bell called Finn Faidheach (the *dh* mute), which was made for him by M'Cecht, one of his three smiths,* and which Dr. Reeves informs us in his paper on the Bell of St. Patrick in the "Transactions of Irish Academy," cannot now be identified, having been taken by John de Courcy at the battle of Down, 1177. O'Curry † remarks that this name, Finn Faidheach, seems to have been given by some of St. Patrick's disciples and successors to some of their favourite bells, and mentions a St. M'Creiche who was a contemporary and friend of St. Ailbe, of Imluich, who, going to stop a plague, raised his " Finn Faidheach " ‡ (*Anglice*, sweet-sounding), on seeing a number of his kinsmen dead of the sickness.

Supposing Fillan to have had this bell, or one so named, the name of Killin is at once explained. Nearly contemporary with Ailbe, having died in 547, Maelgwn was King of Gwynedd, North Wales ; and he is identified with one of the British kings mentioned, under the name of Maglocunus,§ by Gildas, who died in 570. Here we have on the direct route which Fillan would take, if travelling by land between Leinster and the centre of Alba, a king whose names are capable of but one translation. *Mael* is very commonly translated a devotee ; *gwn*, we have seen, is the Welsh of Finn, therefore

* O'Curry, p. 337.                           † p. 630.
‡ Modern—*bhinn*, true, sweet, melodious.   O'Don. O'Reilly's Irish Dict.
Dean of Lismore, p. 58, for bhinn, wynn.
§ Called " Dragon of the Isles," from the ravages perpetrated by him there.

Maelgwn means the devotee of the Finn (faidheach), while Maglocunus is compounded of the words *Mac*, a son, and *clocca*, a bell,
the modern Gaelic clog or clag, Maccloganus, the son of the Bell.*

I have not been able to ascertain whether the aforesaid
M'Creiche ever was in Wales.

The first Fillan has been described as the Stammerer, while,
curiously, the second Fillan is described as having been born with a
stone in his mouth, and is said to have passed the first year of his
life in a pool of water, where he was thrown by his father in con-
tempt. This seems simply an allegory relating the recovery of the
relics of the first Fillan, the bell *Finn Faidheach* and his altar-
stone, a stone which, without impropriety, might be called the
Leac Fail, the slab of Fillan.

We have now appearing in tradition for the first time, about
the beginning of the eighth century, the period at which the second
Fillan flourished, what may have become the "Stone of Destiny"
of Scotland.

Mr. W. F. Skene has, in his little book on the "Stone of
Destiny," given a succinct account of the literature as to its
pretensions, and concludes by proving from the quality of the
stone that it had been quarried in the neighbourhood of Scone, and
never left that place till it was carried off by Edward Longshanks.†

Skene says the first notice of the Stone of Destiny is in
Baldred Bisset's "Processus contra figmenta regis Anglie," compiled in 1301 ; and giving the original "instructions" from which
the "Processus" was compiled, shows there was no mention of the
stone in them. When reduced to a matter-of-fact statement,
Bisset's account of it is that the stone had been brought from Erin
to Scone, having previously been in possession of the Scots.‡

* "Names from personal peculiarities were common, and the possession
of certain relics undoubtedly gave rise to names. The Irish St. Mactail has
his name translated filius asciæ (son of an adze), not because he was a carpenter
(Mac an t-saoir, M'Intyre, called after St. Ciaran), but on the same principle
that Maccaille is filius veli. St. Macnisse of Conor is said to have derived his
name from Mac cnir (Patraic), the son of Patrick's skin, because he slept in
his bed."—Reeves' "Adamn. St. Columba," pp. 237, 238.

† "The kings of Scotland, first of the Pictish monarchy, and afterwards of
the Scottish kingdoms which succeeded it, were inaugurated on this stone,
which was never anywhere but at Scone, the sedes principalis both of the
Pictish and of the Scottish kingdoms."—"Stone of Destiny," p. 44.

‡ "The daughter of Pharaoh, King of Egypt, with an armed band and a large

The Scots who settled in Argyle in 501 were driven out of Alba in 741, when Aengus the Pict took Dunadd, and drove the two branches of its people to extremity,—the Cinel Loarn (family of Lorn), under Muredach, and the Cinel Gabhran, under Alpin, brother of Eochaidh; "for the former appear to have burst from Dalriada upon the Picts who inhabited the Plain of Manann, between the Carron and the Avon," where they were defeated by Talorgan, Aengus's brother; Alpin, with the Cinel Gabhran, invading Galloway, where he was slain.*

Previous to the temporary overthrow of the Scots, however, Nectan the Pict, in the year 717, had driven the Columban clergy over Druim Albain—*i.e.*, into the western part of Alba—having founded a church at Scone; and it was from this date that Scone became the principal seat of the Pictish government.†

Here, then, we have evidence of a quarrel between the King of Picts and the Irish-Scotic clergy about the time of the second Fillan, himself an Irishman, and of the Scotic clergy being driven to the west of Alba; and, curiously enough, we have a trace of the bell, though not of the saint, in Islay.

This island, which became the chief seat of the Lords of the Isles, has, in a loch called Loch Finn-lagan, the remains of a chapel dedicated to a Saint Finn-lagan, of whom there is no mention in any historical record, nor indeed even a tradition. Here, latterly, the Macdonalds were consecrated Lords of the Isles on a large stone, while there was a stone table at which this chief's council sat, and a stone seat for himself. The table and stone seat were carried off by an Earl of Argyle, who, at the same time, removed the bells from Iona.‡

This chapel may be so called from Finn-clagan (*clagan*, a small bell), carried off as a precious relic by the Columban clergy before their expulsion from Pictish territory; and if St. Fillan's stone and

---

fleet, goes to Ireland, and there being joined by a body of Irish, she sails to Scotland, taking with her the royal seat, which he, the King of England, with other insignia of the kingdom of Scotland, carried with him by violence to England. She conquered and destroyed the Picts and their kingdom; and from this Scota, Scotia and the Scots are named."—"Stone of Destiny," p. 19.

  \* " Celtic Scotland," vol. i. p. 290.

  † " Coronation Stone," p. 32.

  ‡ " Origines Parochiales," New Stat. Account, p. 669.

bell had already become connected with the Pictish monarchy, a desire to remove them from Rath Erann or from Glendochart, to Scone, seems a reasonable cause of quarrel between Nectan and the Scoto-Irish clerics.

Lagan, however, is not an impossible spelling of *leacan*, slabs ; and Finn-lagan may most probably have been used as applying both to the bell and altar-stone.

In his " Lectures on the Materials of Irish History," O'Curry gives us the earliest notices of the " La\* Fail." They are contained, First, in the Bàile Chuin—that is, Conn's Prophecy, " Conn of hundred fights," from whom the northern part of Ireland was called " Conn's half," and who was slain A.D. 157,† at the battle of Tuath Amrois, supposed to be near Tara, in Meath. He is the traditional ancestor of the MacDougalls and their allied clans. Second, in the " Bàile an Scail "—the Champion's Ecstasy—to a copy of which, in the British Museum MS., the following history is attached.‡

Conn is described as walking out, accompanied by his three Druids, when he puts his foot on a stone, which shrieked so as to be heard over all East Meath. After consideration, they inform him, " Fal is the name of that stone; it came from Inis Fáil, or the island of Fal ; it has shrieked under your royal feet, and the number of shrieks which the stone has given forth is the number of kings of your seed, that will succeed you to the end of time."

A " knight," describing himself as " one of Adam's race returned from the dead," whose name was Lugh Mac Ceithlenn (Swift, son of *Ceith* of swords), now appears and narrates the names of his successors.

" The prophecy is continued," says O'Curry, " down to the monarch Fergus, son of Maclduin, who was to be slain in the battle of Almhain, on a Friday, an occurrence which took place in the year 718. And here our copy unfortunately breaks off, otherwise we should be pretty well able to fix the probable date of the original composition of this piece."

---

\* " *a* was sometimes written for *ea* of the moderns." Remarks on letter *a*, O'Don. O'Reilly's Dictionary.

† " Annals of the Four Masters."

‡ O'Curry, p. 387.

If Mac Ceith brought the La Fail with him from Scotland, which is part at least of the island of Fail (in other words, Britain), in 717, 718 would be the first year in which it could prophecy after the event in Ireland.

I would now direct attention to a story printed for the first time in J. F. Campbell of Islay's "Tales of the West Highlands," published in 1860, and narrated to him by a blind fiddler, James Wilson, in Islay, and by John Campbell, Strath Gearloch, in Ross-shire.

A brief extract of both versions is as follows.*

The Ceabharnach (Champion ; Catheran, as it is used in the Low country) starts from Islay, from Loch Aird an Uamha,† Loch Thorabais,‡ and Loch Phort an Eillean,§ another name for Loch Finlagane, and by sixteen steps he reaches Ireland.

> " He moved as sea heaps from sea heaps,
> And as playballs from playballs,
> As a furious winter wind,
> So swiftly, sprucely, cheerily,
> Right proudly
> Through glens and high tops,
> And no stop made he till he came
> To city and court of O'Domhnuill."

He tells O'Domhnuill whence he came.

> " I came from hurry scurry,
> From the end of endless spring,
> From the loved swanny glen,
> A night in Islay and a night in Man,
> A night on cold watching cairns,
> On the face of a mountain.
> In the Scotch king's town was I born.
> A soiled sorry Champion am I,
> Though I happened on this town."

O'Domhnuill, who is disgusted at so sorry a fellow having passed his doorkeeper, asks him what he can do.   The Champion shows himself to be a much greater artist than O'Domhnuill's harpers, for he either plays the Irish performers into a profound sleep by the power of his music, so that none could waken them ;

---

* Campbell's "Tales," vol. i. p. 289.      ‡ Mound of Death.
† Hill of the grave.      § Harbour Island.

or breaks their harps, so as to make them utterly useless; then sets the men on their legs again, or repairs their harps by his skill as a physician. He then visits Seathan Mor Mac an t-Iarla deas (Seathan Mohr, son of the Southern Earl), where he again shows his miraculous healing powers, calling himself Duradan o Duradan (Dust of Dust).

According to the second version, he now visits the Man of Munster, where he kills his guards and his doorkeeper, and plays various tricks on him, but ultimately puts all to rights.

Then he visits a person styled in version No. 1 the Bodach (old fellow) M'Ceochd, and in No. 2, Rob M'Sheoic ic a Lagain, *i.e.*, Robert M'Sheoic MacLagan. This potentate had been lame for seven years, and had been treated, without success, by all the physicians of Ireland; but Gille an Leigh (the Leech's lad; the *gh* is mute), as the Champion now calls himself, cures the "Bodach" of his incapacity of motion, and makes him swifter of foot than any of his physicians. After refusing Maclagan's daughter as a wife, and an offer of the post of assistant and successor to Rob himself, he goes to O'Connachar Sligeach—*i.e.*, O'Connachar of Sligo (version No. 1), Taog O'Ceallaidh (version No. 2)—and accompanies them when they were going to "raise the spoil" of the Cailliche Buidhniche, but on the condition of being treated as an equal.* This condition not being fulfilled, he returns, after this freebooting expedition, to be choked, by the daughter of M'Ceochd, with a drink of warm milk and green apples.

The points in this which first catch the attention are the prominent part played by a Gille an Leigh, the pronunciation of which conveys the meaning either of the "physician's lad," or the "lad of the stone" (Mac Lea), and a MacLagan, who is called Rob, the son of a person of the name M'Ceochd, somewhat similar to that of St. Patrick's smith, M'Ceith, and the father of the ghostly warrior of the Bàile an Scail; while the special attributes shared betwixt them are, sweetness of their music, swiftness of foot, and a miraculous power of healing.

Let us compare with the above the so-called prophecy—*i.e.*, really a narrative of past events put in the form of a prophecy, and contained in the Life of St. Cadroe.†

* As he had been by Murchadh Mac Brian (version 2).
† "Chron. Picts and Scots," preface, p. 41.

Skene tells us that the Dalriadic Kingdom (the first kingdom of the Scots in Scotland) lasted from the commencement of the fifth to the middle of the eighth century, and between Alpin, the last king of Dalriada, and Kenneth MacAlpin, the first king of the latter Scottish kingdom, an interval of a century occurs in the lists of kings given by the early chroniclers (those, that is to say, who wrote before the eleventh century,) during which period Angus MacFergus the Pict, founded St. Andrews and established a Pictish kingdom in Dalriada.

Kenneth MacAlpin obtained possession of Scone in 850, and died in 860. St. Berchan says the Scots whom Kenneth led were not the colony which founded Dalriada, but that they came out of Galloway, where they had lived with the Picts, and from which they spread into Argyle and the Isles. On the other hand, St. Cadroe's Life gives the following remarkable account of the Scottish wanderings, which is different from all others.* They are there said to enter Ireland, to obtain possession of Cloyne (in Cork), then Armagh and the whole country between Loch Earn and Loch Neagh, then Kildare and Cork, and finally to enter Benchor (Bangor) in Ulster. Then after the expiration of many years they pass over into Iona, and proceed by the River Rossis to occupy the region of Rossia, and finally to possess the cities of Rigmonadh (St. Andrews †) and Bellathor (Scone †). May this latter not be Logierait? Skene says this legend seems to indicate the progress of an ecclesiastical party, and he identifies Rossia with the province of Ross, the Rossis with Rasay, the old name of the Blackwater, which runs from Loch Droma through the long valley from near the head of Loch Broom to fall into the Conan at Contin, near Dingwall. Skene further points out that Hector Boece mentions a colony of Scots, who were said to have been led by a "Redda" (Scalachronica), "Rether" (Fordun), in a direction which exactly corresponds with the line of that invasion given in the Life of Cadroe. Skene says that this leader passed from Ireland into the Hebrides, and having collected forces in Albion, entered Loch Broom, and proceeding to the south, arrived at Dingwall, and thence penetrated into the south of Britain.

* "Chron. Picts and Scots," pp. 183, 188, 191, 193.
† "Coronation Stone."

The following is a tabulated comparison of Mr. Campbell's story and St. Cadroe's prophecy, with events and dates mentioned in the "Annals of the Four Masters":—

| CADROE'S "LIFE." | "ANNALS OF THE FOUR MASTERS." | CAMPBELL'S "CEATHARNACH." |
|---|---|---|
| | Domhnall, son of Murchad, King of Ireland, 739 to 758. | Ceatharnach goes to O'Donill's country. |
| Go to Cloyne, which is in Cork. | ...... | Ceatharnach goes to Seathan Mor, the son of the Southern Earl, and is next seen "13 miles on the west side of Limerick. |
| Armagh. | Forannan (see p. 17), Primate of Ardmacha, was taken prisoner by the foreigners at Cluain-Comharda with his *relics* and people, and they were carried by them to their ships at Luimneach (Limerick). At this time the foreigners (Gall) also plundered Connaught and Meath, 843. | ...... |
| | Gilla Mac Liagh, Primate of Armagh before 1173. (O'Curry, p. 361.) Latinised Gelasius, *i.e.*, Gille an Lea sius. | ...... |
| Loch Neagh. | Gallaibh. Foreigners in Loch Neagh, 838. | ...... |
| Kildare. | Olchobar, King of Munster, Lorcan, son of Ceallach, defeat the foreigners at Sciath Nechtain, in Kildare, 846. | Ceatharnach goes to Man of Munster. |
| Cork. | ...... | ...... |
| ...... | Doonfeeny. Rath Lacken, in Sligo, in district afterwards called Laggan, of which an O'Murray was chief. Slain 1267. | Bodach ic Ceochd ic Lagain. |
| Bangor in Ulster. | ...... | ...... |
| ...... | The plundering of Colooney, in Sligo, by the fleet of the Cailli, 844, and their subsequent defeat. | O'Connach Sligeach and Taog O'Ceallaidh lift the prey of the Cailliche Buidhniche. |

Bearing in mind the connection with the ravages of the so-called strangers, those who read Campbell's story will notice the mention of the galloglachs (the foreign youth), commonly spoken of as gallow glasses.—*Vide* "Macbeth," *Act. 1, Scene 2.*

Besides the coincidences in narrative, it is evident from the above-quoted fragments of poetry that the Champion travelled by sea ; while, in support of the statement that he passed one night in Islay and one in Man, we have the circumstance of the existence of "Loch Finn-lagan," in Islay, and the record of the defeat by the Picts of "Cinel Loarn" (family of Lorn), under Muredach, in the plain of "Manan," after they had been driven out of Argyle.

But it is not alone in Islay we have a Finn-lagan, but in Ireland also, and in Connaught we find the same designatory terms, but applied separately.

On the side of Killala Bay, farthest from Sligo, is a smaller bay called Lacken Bay, where we find Rath Lacken (the fort of the slab), and close to it Doonfeeny (the fort " Dun " of Finn). The district in which these places are, is mentioned in the "Annals of the Four Masters," in 1267, as under the name of Laggan, in possession of a chief of Laggan called O'Murray. Here, I think, there is every probability that the Finn Faidheach and the La Fail found a resting-place during part of the time of Rob M'Ceochd's lameness.*

Having landed our pilgrims at Scone, and being on the border-land between tradition and history, there are still one or two matters of significance in tradition to which attention should be directed.

Rob M'Cheoic's swiftness of foot was an attribute of all others which one would scarcely expect to find connected with either a bell or a stone ; but we have seen that the champion of the La Fail also called himself " Swift," and as he reports himself to have returned from the dead A.D. 718, historical notice of his existence in ordinary mortal frame must be looked for before that date.

Now, Maelgwn, *alias* Maglocunus, is known by another name, Meilchon Mailcunus,† and this name is translated "miolchu," the greyhound,‡ and in the "Martyrology of Donegal" we have several saints of whose names an integral part is the epithet "swift."

1. Luightighern (*the swift Lord*) mac Ua Trato (the son of

* Seven years, the time he is said to have been unable to move, is a well-known figurative expression used in Scripture ; and in modern Gaelic, *seachd sgith*, seven tired—*i.e.*, excessively tired.

† " Chron. Picts and Scots," p. 12.

‡ Among the crests said to have been used by some Maclagans the greyhound is one.

O'Trato), who is at Tuaim (*i.e.*, buried or venerated there), Finn Locha, in Tratraighe. Brigh, daughter of Forannan, son of Conull, son of Tochtan, son of Amhalgaidh, sister of Maelaithghin, was his mother.

2. Finnlugh (Swift Finn). There are four of this name. The days of their commemoration are the only particulars given in two of these cases ; of the third, who was commemorated on the 5th June at Cluain mic Feig (doubtless Magh Feci, in Bregia,* East Meath), we have this further particular, that mention is made of a companion of his bearing the suggestive name of Brogán (shoes); while the fourth is described as of Tamhlacht-Finnlogha (*i.e.*, the resting-slab of Swift Finn), in Cinnachta Glinne Geimhin, which is in Ulster.

This last had a blood relation, the notice of whom is as follows (p. 317) :—

"Septimo Kal Decembris (25th Nov.)

"Finnchu, son of Fionnlogh of Bri-Gobhann, in Fir-Maithe-Feine, in Munster. He is of the race of Brian, son of Eochaidh Muigh-medhoin (*i.e.*, Fionnlogh, son of Sedna), and Idnait, daughter of Flann-lethderg of the Cinneachta of Glen-Geimhin, was his mother, as the Book of Mac Carthaigh Riabhach states (commonly called the Book of Lismore). It was Ailbe of Imleach Iubhair that baptized him. Fionnchu was seven years in the abbacy of Benchor, next after Comhghall. Life of Finnchu, chap. 5. Fionnchu was a pupil of Comhghall, and it was with him he studied, chap. 4.

"This was the Fionnchu who used often to be in a stone prison not higher than his own length, and a stone over his head and a stone under his feet, and two iron staples under each side of the prison; and he used to rest both his arm-pits on these staples, so that his head might not touch the stone above, nor his feet the stone below. The proof of this is what Cuimin of Coindeire said—

'Fionnchu of Bri-Gobhann loves
The blessing of Jesus on his soul.
Seven years was he on his hooks
Without his touching the ground.'

"Comhghall of Benchor came to him on one occasion and commanded him to come out of the prison, and he obeyed him, though with reluctance, &c. It was he who used to lie the first night in the same grave with every corpse which used to be buried in his church."

---

* "Round Towers," p. 101.

These epithets—"Dog Finn,"* "son of Swift Finn" of the "miracle of the smith," who was baptised by Ailbe, the teacher of Fillan and of M'Criech, who was in Benchor, and left it at the command of Comhghall, the founder of that abbey, in 552—can, it seems to me, only have one origin, viz., the story of the Finn Faidheach ; *i.e.*, the Bell of Maglocunus and of Fillan.   There is, however, I think, a mistake in making the date of Finn's residence at Benchor to be immediately after Comhghall.   Doubtless he was after Comhghall, but not for nearly three centuries.

There are also several saints mentioned in this Martyrology of the names of Molocca, Molacca, and Molaga (*mo*, my ; *clocca*, a bell), and of Moliag and Macliag (*liag*, a stone stab), one MacLiag being bishop at Liathdrum, a name of Teamhair or Tara, in Meath.

There is in the Book of Leinster, a manuscript of *circa* 1100, a list of those said to have suffered martyrdom with St. Donan in Eig, on Sunday, 17th April, 617, among whom appears the name of Macloga.

I feel no little diffidence in approaching anything resting on the basis of an Ogmic inscription, but I cannot avoid referring to two names so like Maclagan that it is difficult to believe that one, at all events, is not the same ; yet Professor Rhys, from whose book, "Lectures on Welsh Philology," I draw my facts, is of the opinion that "Maglagni" is nothing but an ancient spelling of Maelgwn.

There is at Llanfechan, near Llanbyther in Cardigan, a stone inscribed in Ogmic and Latin—"Hic jacet Trennecathus filius Maglagni."   The translation of Trennecathus (bold in battle) seems to present but little difficulty to one moderately acquainted with Gaelic, nor indeed does the translation of the other name.   But, if I understand him aright, Mr. Rhys takes as his starting-point Maelgwn and Maglocunus to be the same name ; cites a stone at Ballintaggart, Ireland, inscribed in Ogmic, " tria maqua Mailagni," on which stone is marked a cross ; quotes the Ogmic word " Magli " (p. 387), which he says is Mael, or Irish Màl, equivalent to a prince, noble, or king, and by a process of philological analysis, changing *g* into *e* before *n* in modern Welsh, simplifying (?) the termination *agn* into *angn*, and still further into *an*, he transmo-

---

* *Miol* is a word applied to any animal, a louse, &c.   Miolgwn (Maelgwn) would then be the animal of Finn, the dog Finn, Finnchu.

grifies Maglagn into Maelan, which he says is the modern equivalent of Maelgwn—Maglagn, the Maglocunus of Gildas, surviving in the name Garth-Maclan. I have pointed out what seems the simple translation of Maglocunus and Maelgwn, and I have no doubt that Maglagni is the same word as the former of these. Mailagni is not so clear, but while noticing the cross on the stone, and its situation at the " Priest's town," as evidence of its Christian origin, I would suggest the following as a probable parallel and explanation :—

In the Dean of Lismore's Book (p. 32), in the old Gaelic of an Ossianic poem, which (p. 43) is said to be " remarkable, and bears decided marks of genuineness and antiquity, the language peculiar, and many of the words obsolete," we have " Math Morn is dane," which Dr. MacLachlan translates into modern Gaelic, —" Mac Moirne is deine," Mac Morn more brave. But there is a use of *math*, good, for a noble—as, *maithean*, noblemen; * a custom still surviving in the expression " the gudeman," applied to the head of a family ; and as in this case the stone is to the memory of three sons of " Mailagni," they may not impossibly have been sons of the nobles of Leinster—Lagen, Lagenia being the name given to Leinster in the lives of the Saints.† As a proper name applied to one individual, I believe we have Mailagni several times in the " Martyrology of Donegal " as Maelaithghein, a saint of this name being Bishop of Moville, in Donegal; another being described as of Tigh Maelaithghein, in the west of Bregia, which is in Leinster. In the " Annals of the Four Masters," under the year of the world 4606, the name of Leinster is said to be derived from " Laighne," a sort of broad-headed spear introduced into Ireland by Moen, Mael-laighne (the devotee of the spear ?).

If one may risk a conjecture, the names of the King of Gwynedd —Meilchon, Maelgwyn—may have arisen thus. The greyhound was his heathen name, the devotee of the bell his baptismal name, and this was Latinised into Maglocunus by Gildas. The relationship of Luightighern by his mother's side with Maelaithghein is quite compatible with the first Fillan's Leinster parentage.

If my inferences are correct, we have brought the bell from Wales to Scotland, followed the bell and stone from Scotland

* Mithean' us maithean an t-sluaigh—*i.e.*, rabble and nobles.
† Camden's " Britannia," p. 68.

to Ireland, and back again from Ireland through the Isles and
north of Scotland to Scone; and it is an undoubted historic fact,
that there was a stone at Scone with a traditional history attached
to it of such consequence as to make the King of England carry
it off in the end of the thirteenth century, which stone is now in
Westminster Abbey.

Dr. Stuart, in his account of the Staff of St. Fillan in the
"Proceedings of the Society of Antiquaries, 1877," p. 138, tells us
that Edward I. at the same time carried off the "bell and bachull
(crosier) of the unknown saint of the Stone of Destiny," quoting from
Mr. Joseph Robertson. This quotation I have been unable to verify.

That this unknown saint was St. Fillan seems clear, but his bell
and staff are both now in Scotland; and, except the above statement, there is no evidence to prove their having gone to England
with the stone; while a well-known Gaelic proverb, which I give
as Dr. M'Leod, of St. Columba's, Glasgow, wrote it in his "Caraid
nan Gaidheal," proves the presence of a bell of some notoriety at
Scone,—"Mar thuirt Clag Scain, an rud nach buin duit, na buin
dà"—that is, "As says the Bell of Scone, what does not belong
to you, don't meddle with it."

In connection with this, it is to be noticed that, in the reign of
William the Lyon (1165 to 1214), the name of the first judex of
Gowrie is recorded as Macbeth,[*] several of the name appearing
in the reign of David I. (1124 to 1153), one of them being Thane
of Falkland, a position equivalent to that of a feu-holder direct
from the Crown, but not necessarily of much dignity. This name
naturally leads to the consideration of the Macbeth made known
to everybody by Shakespeare.

There is a genuine old Gaelic manuscript written in 1467, now
in the Advocates' Library, supposed to be part of the collection
long preserved by the family of MacLachlan of Kilbride,[†] in which
is Macbeth's genealogy, traceable by joining on to the short
notice of Macbeth himself the genealogies preceding it where we
find the common ancestor. It is as follows[‡]:—"Macbiad mc
*Finnleic*, mc Ruadiri mc Donaill mc Morgan (here commences
genealogy of rulers of Moray), mc Donaill mc Catmael *mc Ruadiri*

---

* "Caledonia," vol. i. p. 412.
† *The Gael*, 1877, p. 27.
‡ *The Gael*, 1876, p. 368.

mc Aircellach mc Fearchair Fata mc Fearadaigh mc Fergusa mc
Sneachtain mc Colman mc Buadan mc Eachach mc Maredaig
*Mc Loarn mor* (here commences King David's pedigree), *Mc Eirc*
mc Eachach muinreamhair mc Aengusa mc Feilime mc Seancormac
mc *Cruitenithe mc Finnfeiche*," and so back to Adam; but having
reached an ancestor bearing the name Cruitenithe (*i.e.*, Pict), son of
"Finn Faidheach," we may rest content, and take the rest on
trust.   I have put in italics the ancestors who seem to be land-
marks in this inquiry; and we find, coming from the more ancient
downwards, that Macbeth was a descendant of Loarn Mor, the
son of Erc, from whom were descended the Cinel Lorn.

We have seen the Scots led through Scotland from the Isles by
a Rether, which is doubtless the same name as Rydderich ("red
king," ri dearg) of the Strathclyde Britons, while eight generations
back from Macbeth we have the Gaelic equivalent of it—Ruadiri
(ruadh ri), who is made the son of Aircellach, the last Dalriadic
king of the Cinel Loarn.*   Now, eight back in the genealogy of
Duncan, Macbeth's contemporary, we have Kenneth, who is made
the son of Alpin, the last of the Dalriadic kings of the Cinel
Gabran, a hiatus thus occurring in both these pedigrees during
the wanderings in Ireland, and making the identification of
Ruadiri and Rether the more probable.   Macbeth's father was
Finnlay, the latter part of whose name was divided from the first
syllable by the Irish chroniclers, and he is described as Fin Mic
Laig, which Skene † says was done to suit Irish traditions.   Finnlay
was Maormor of Ross, and was in all probability the Finleik Scota
Jarl mentioned in Claf Trygveson's Saga as the antagonist of
Sigurd, at the end of the tenth century, before Sigurd married the
daughter of Malcolm II.‡   What the Irish traditions are to
which Skene alludes I am not certain, but I think the name has
some connection with the La Fail.   There is a clan in Ross-shire,
Mac Lea, who claim descent from Ferchard Leche (*i.e.*, Ferchard
Beathad, Beaton or Bethune), § who was physician to Robert II.,
and had from him grants of land in Sutherlandshire, in 1379.

* Boece makes the Murrays come to Scotland under command of a Roderick.
—Bellenden's Boece, vol. i. p. 123.
  † "Chron. Picts and Scots," preface, p. 32.
  ‡ Chal. "Caledonia," vol. i. p. 406.
  § "Trans. Soc. Antiq.," vol. xii. pt. ii. p. 547.

That there exists a family whose commencement dates only from the end of the fourteenth century, bearing the name of MacLeigh, "the son of the physician," is believed, but the name must be much older than that.    In the " New Statistical Account," *sub voce* Contin, there is mentioned as in Loch Achilty, in that parish, an island, "supposed to be artificial, which belonged to M'Lea Mor, who possessed a large extent of property in the parish, and who was wont in seasons of danger to retire to the island as a place of refuge from his enemies.    The ruins of his dwelling are still to be traced.    A niche was long seen in the wall which was called Cruist Mhic a Lea, from its having formed part of a vault in which that family was buried."    The Great M'Lea who had his castle on an artificial island was surely alive before Ferchard the king's leech, and seems to me more likely to be the opponent of Sigurd and the father of Macbeth than a Highland robber of later times ; while the niche, part of a vault in which the family were buried, may or may not have been a resting-place of a kinsman, Rob Mac Sheoic ic a Lagain.    The "considerable property in the parish" seems represented by Ben Lea, at the side of the Blackwater, the Rossis of Cadroe, about the centre of Ross-shire.

In the list of Macdougalls and their dependants, classed among the latter we have MacLeas, mentioned as improperly calling themselves Livingstones ; and I fancy Ewen MacDougall and Captain Thomas* are at one in holding that the name signifies the son of the Leech ; and this view seems to hold good even if M'Lea Mor were Finnleigh, the Earl of Ross, when his son is called Mac Bheatha, the son of Life, while Robert II.'s physician was also a Macbeth, of whose clan Captain Thomas informs us there are notices in Islay, Mull, and South Uist.    Have we not also corroboration by the story of the Ceatharnach, who was Gille an Leigh, with his miraculous power of healing men and harps ?    And yet I incline to the Livingstone translation as the more correct.

We began with the Finn Faidheach, the sweet-sounding bell ; we picked up the stone called La Fail, which sounded under the feet of Conn, and thus became the La Faidheach ; the *bh* in Gaelic sounding *v*, Lea Bheathach (bheathaidh) would thus be equivalent to, Living stone ; Mac Faidhich, the son (gen.) of Faidheach ;

---

* " Trans. Soc. Antiq.," *supra* cited.

Mac Bheatha, the son of Life,* becoming a proper name. Macbeda, Macbethad, Macbrethach, Macbeth.

Bishop Forbes notices on the handle of the Bell of St. Fillan the well-known symbol of the phallus, an emblem said to have been carried by the Egyptians at the feast of Osiris, as well as by other nations in religious ceremonies. " Phallus," says Dr. Forbes,† "from Bal, a strength (Sanscrit), was the symbol of health, life, and regeneration, and thus attributed to Baal. Modern Gaelic, Ball, a limb, member, *membrum virile.* Ballan, a cow's teat; ballan ioch shlaint, a charm-draught, a cordial. While in Irish, *biach* is the male organ, glossed in O'Reilly "ball feardha," *i.e.*, the male member.

Mr. Anderson, of the Antiquarian Museum, kindly pointed out to me that the handle where joined to the bell is divided as if to represent the jaws of an animal, while the lateral protuberances represented eyes, and the central one its crest, an exceedingly common device in the joining of handles in old castings, the crest being frequently present and often much prolonged. Beath is also Gaelic for a living creature, also beathach, and beathadhach, this latter specially meaning a beaver, while the adjective beathrach is translated as, "of a serpent." It is at least curious to notice that Bishop Forbes believed that he had recognised the phallus here, totally unconnected with any idea of a connection between the bell and the name MacBeth.

Nor are Finlay and Macbeth the only names in this family having an etymological connection with what has been already mentioned. For Macbeth married the widow of his cousin Gilcomgain, recalling the name of the saint whom the second Fillan succeeded at Glendochart, and of the one who ordered Finnchu out of his stone chest at Benchor, while Gilcomgain's son, who afterwards was Maormor of Moray, was called Lulach, the swift hero.

---

* Remarks on letter *b*, O'Donovan's O'Reilly's Dictionary. "By putting a tittle or point over this letter in Irish (which is a late invention not to be found in any old parchments) it sounds like the Latin *v* consonant, as we have no such letter in our alphabet, which is the case of the Greeks, though their *b* or *beta* is often rendered in Latin by *v*, Greek *biote*, Latin *vita*, Irish *beatha*, and when tittled it sounds *veatha*, vita." The letter *h* is used in Scotch Gaelic instead of the tittle. Irish *b*, Scottish *bh*. Under letter *f* Dr. O'Brien remarks, when a tittled or aspirated *b* is prefixed to *f* it is pronounced like *v* consonant; thus, a b̔fuaire is pronounced *a vuaire*."

† " Proceed. Soc. Antiq.," vol. viii. pt. ii. p. 373.

That Macbeth reigned from end to end of the ground traversed by the ecclesiastical party of St. Cadroe's prophecy, as chief of Ross and Moray, and king of Scotland, is itself a presumption in favour of his having had some claim to a seat on the Stone of Destiny, while the claim of the kings of Scotland to be able to cure scrofula seems likely to be connected with the traditional leprosy of Fillan and the healing powers of the sweet-sounding bell.

The connection between St. Fillan and the Scottish kings continued even subsequently to the removal of the Stone of Destiny to England. We have Robert I. giving the custody of Fillan's crosier to the Dewars—Bruce, who died of leprosy, having had possibly a personal interest in a saint who was himself so afflicted; and even so lately as 1488 it is recorded that James IV., who was crowned at Scone in June of that year, had St. Fillan's bell brought to his coronation.*

In 1798 an acquisitive gentleman visiting Glendochart carried off the bell to England. In his account of this deed of his, he tells us how the people of the neighbourhood treated lunatics, the ceremony being a kind of travesty of a coronation. The unfortunate patient was thrown into St. Fillan's pool, with a rope tied round him, and after being drawn out, he was taken to the top of an adjacent knoll, on which was St. Fillan's seat, tied into a wooden frame thereon, crowned with the bell, and left till morning, when, if he was found loose, he was considered as cured.†

The Gaelic for a helmet is *clogad*, which, on the authority of Shaw, quoted in O'Donovan's O'Reilly's Irish Dictionary, who gives *ada* as meaning victory, may be translated *clog ada*, the bell of victory; while the form of the helmets on Highland engraved stones suggests the use of a name describing them in nearly the words of the modern schoolboy, when he speaks of wearing what he calls his bell topper. When taken to the coronation of James IV., the bell may have been brought from Killin, but it does not seem to have been the opinion of the people that it had always been there, for they said St. Fillan caused it to fly to the church there, and a soldier seeing it in the air, fired at it and brought it down.‡    This traditional soldier was, to judge from his

---

* " Proceed. Soc. Antiq., 1877," p. 148.
† " Proceed. Soc. Antiq., 1877," p. 148.
‡ " Proceed. Soc. Antiq., 1870," p. 267.

equipment, of a date posterior to Robert Bruce; but the story, ridiculous as it is, points to a capture of the bell having been made at some time or in some way or other.

Mr. Campbell tells us that in Barra * he was told that the *ord Finn* (the hammer of Finn) was a bell which was not to be struck but "in time of great rejoicing, or in time of hard straits; and that it could be heard over the five-fifths of Erin."†

Having avoided the collecting of traditions from my own clansmen till I thought I had some light on the subject, it was not till after I had noted much of what is written above that I got the story of the Macandrossers ‡ (p. 6) and the Lorn Brooch, though it had been casually mentioned to me before, only to be rejected as quite without significance. I quote Barbour's account of the combat with the Bruce from Dr. Stuart's paper on the Crosier of St. Fillan,§ and according to it none of the assailants escaped alive.

---

* "Tales of West Highlands," vol. iii. p. 304.

† A curious mixture of the traditions of Thor, Mac Cumhail, and the Finn Faidheach, suggesting that further inquiry will yet unravel much as to the probable history of the leader of the Feinn.

‡ Macandorsair—*i.e.*, son of the doorkeeper.

§ " For the king full chevelrously
  Defendit all his cumpany,
  And was set in full gret danger,
  And yhet eschapit hale and fer.
  For twa brethir war in that land
  That war the hardyast of hand
  That war intill all that cuntre,
  And tha had sworn, gif tha micht se
  The Brus quhar tha micht him ourta
  That tha suld de or than him sla.
  Thar surnam was Makyndrosser
  That is all sa mekill to say her
  As the Durwarth sonnis perfay :
  Of thar covyn the thrid had tha
  That was richt stout, ill, and feloun.
  Quhen tha the king of gud renoun
  Saw sa behind his menyhe rid,
  And saw him turn so many tid,
  Tha abad quhill that he was
  Enterit in ane narow plas
  Betuix ane lochside and ane bra
  That was sa strat, I undirta,
  That he micht nocht wele turn his sted.
  Than with ane will till him tha yhed

But in the story of the Champion (p. 12) the doorkeepers play a prominent part, and that the office was one of importance is proved by the fact that in the household of the King of Connaught, in 1224, the doorkeeper is ranked before the historian, physician, and brehon (judge), though junior to the chief butler.*

About the same date there were two Earls of Athol, Thomas of Galloway, Comes Atholiae, and Allanus Ostiarius regis (king's doorkeeper) Comes Atholiae, the latter making a grant of the

> And ane him be the brydill hynt,
> Bot he raucht till him sic ane dint
> That arm and schuldir flaw him fra.
> With that ane othir can him ta
> Be the leg, and his hand can schut
> Betuix the sterap and his fut
> And, quhen the king feld thar his hand,
> In his sterapis stithly can he stand,
> And strak with spuris the sted in hy,
> And he lansit furth deliverly,
> Sa that the tothir falyheit fet,
> And nocht forthi his hand was yhet
> Undir the sterap magre his.
> The thrid with full gret hy with this
> Richt to the bra-sid he yhed,
> And stert behind him on his sted.
> The king was than in full gret pres ;
> The quhethir he thocht, as he that wes
> In all his dedis avise,
> To do ane outrageous bounte.
> He hynt him that behind him was,
> And magre his him can he ras
> Fra behind him, thouch he had sworn
> And laid him evin him beforn,
> Syn with the suerd sic dint him gaf
> That he the hed to the harnis claf.
> He ruschit doun of blud all red
> As he that stound feld of ded
> And than the king in full gret hy
> Strak at the tothir vigorously
> That he eftir his sterap drew,
> That at the first strak he him slew,
> On this wis him deliverit he
> Of all tha feloun fais thre."
>
> " Proceed. Soc. Antiq., 1877," p. 145.

---

* " Sculptured Stones of Scotland," vol. ii. p. 52.

wood of *Terpheach*,* previously granted by Thomas of Lundin, "ostiarius regis pater suus," which grant was ratified by Alexander in a charter of 12th October, 19 of his reign (A.D. 1233).

Logierait is in the beginning of the same century, under the name of Logy Mached in Athol, confirmed to Scone monastery by John, Bishop of Dunkeld, "with pertinents,—viz., Le Rath, which is the head of the county and of the whole Thanedom of Dul monych (Dull), and of the whole Thanedom of Fandufuith."†

Here, then, we have the Durwards (a Fife family), Earls of Athol, of which county Logie Rath was the head, before the time of the Bruce, the other Earl of Athol being most likely a MacDougall, as in 1190 Rolland MacDoual is called Princeps Gallovidiæ.‡

Now, Thomas was Earl of Athol in right of his wife, Allan the doorkeeper being married to a co-heiress, the earldom of Athol at this time apparently going out of the direct line. And let us notice here that these two families of MacDougall and Durward being partisans of Edward I., it seems probable that he would hand over to them the Bell of the Stone of Destiny if they claimed an hereditary right to its custody.

In one of the laws of William the Lyon (1165 to 1214), however, called "Claremathane" (apparently composed from the word clare (*clare constat*) and *mo*, my; *thane*, earl), we find the earls of Athol and the abbots of Glendochart sharing the jurisdiction over the dwellers of the adjacent part of Argyle : § "Item si calumpniatus vocaverit warentum aliquem in Ergadia quæ pertinet Scociam, tunc veniat ad comitem Atholiæ vel ad abbatem de Glendochard, et ipsi mittent cum eo homines suos qui testentur supra dictam assisam"—that is, "Also if an informer may have called any warrant in Argyle which pertains to Scotia, then he should go to the Earl of Athole or to the Abbot of Glendochart, and they will send with him their men, who will bear witness upon the same assise."

In the "New Statistical Account," a Gaelic name is given to Logierait, "Bal no maoir,"|| which is there translated the "town of

---

* An old law-paper quoting from the Chartulary of Arbroath, Note-Book, p. 64.
† "Caledonia," vol. i. p. 718.
‡ Chalmers' "Caledonia," vol. iii. p. 372. It is noteworthy that the oldest clans in Galloway are the MacDougalls and M'Clellands, while the Logans are ancient both in Carrick (Southern Ayrshire) and in Ulster.
§ "Celtic Scot," vol. ii. p. 407. "Act Parl.," vol. i. p. 50, now 373 cit.
|| Maor-mheirleach—*i.e.*, thief-taker ; Maor—*i.e.*, a steward, or any officer.

the thief-takers;" though I think, in view of its being the seat of an earldom, it will quite as well bear to be considered as the "town of the stewards." *

Putting, then, together the proverb connected with the Bell of Scone (p. 21), the name Macbeth as the first sheriff of the district in which it was, the Gaelic names of Logierait and the connection of the Maclagans with that locality, with the other circumstances above mentioned,—it is a fair conjecture that at the beginning of the twelfth century, when surnames first came into use, the clan of the Maor or Thane of Athol called themselves "Maclagane," and the clan of the abbots of Glendochart Mac an abbane, Macnab,† as attached to the earldom of Athol and the abbacy of Glendochart respectively. When Robert Bruce granted the Dewars the custody of St. Fillan's Crosier he gave them certain of the duties of the earls of Athol, as above mentioned—"If it happened that any goods or cattle were stolen or carried off from any one dwelling in Glendochart, and he from whom they were taken, whether from doubt of the culprit, or from the feud of his enemies, did not dare to follow after his property, then he should send a messenger to the said Jore of the Cogerach, with fourpence or a pair of shoes, with food for the first night, and then the said Jore, on his own charges, ought to follow the said cattle wherever they were to be found within the kingdom of Scotland." ‡ I would call special attention here to the practical character in which St. Finnlugh's companion, Brogán (shoes) of Donegal, here seems to present himself (p. 17).

It may be noted that the bells of St. Lolan and St. Kessog, Bishop Forbes tells us, were included in the feudal investiture of

---

* " Not lang efter, he [*i.e.*, Walter Stewart] was send with ane gret power in the Ilis, Galloway, and othir partis of Scotland, to punis tyrannis and limmaris of the cuntre; quhom he dantit with sic manheid and prudence, that he was maid Stewart of Scotland, to resave the kingis malis and rentis out of al partis of the realme."—Bellenden's Boece, vol. ii. p. 265.

† The genealogy of Macnab.—" Do Genelach ic an abhane.—Gillemare ic Eogan ic Aengusa ic ic Biad ic Aengusa ic Gillemare Logaig ic Fearchair ic Finlaic ic Doncesi ic Firtire ic Gillafaelan ic Gillamart ic Firtead ic Loairn ic Fearchair ic Cormaic mc Oirbertaig ic Eirc ic Donaill duin ic Fearchar abradh ruaidh ic Fearadaig," &c. The second last being apparently Fearchar fada—*i.e.*, the *tall* or the *red.—The Gael*, 1877, p. 7.

‡ " Proceed. Soc. Antiq., 1877," p. 156.

the earls of Perth.* Of the former saint, who, according to the
"Calendars," may have lived any time from the uncertain period
of Servanus to that of King Duncan, the name has a strong
resemblance to Lellan in M'Lellan, the common spelling of Mac
Gille Fhaelain; while Drummond, the family name of the earls of
Perth, seems derived from Druim Muind, the ridge of St. Mundus,
the instructor of the second Fillan.

Cunedag,† the great-grandfather of Maglocunus, came from
Manau Guotodin, and with his eight sons drove the Scots out of
Guenedote, with great slaughter, 186 years before Maelgwn reigned.
Maelgwn died 547, therefore Cunedag came to Wales about A.D.
361. It is doubtful whether this is history or vague tradition.

Manau, Manand‡ has the name still preserved in the moorland
parish of Slamannan (from the Gaelic Sliabh Mannan, the word
sliabh signifying a moor). It certainly extended as far as the
River Almond, and may possibly have included the whole of the
modern county of Linlithgow; and as this county approaches at
Queensferry within a short distance of the opposite coast of the
Firth, it may have even extended beyond it, and left another trace
of its name in the town of Clackmannan.

In the central part of the district above described we find a
place Torphichen (Tor faidheach? Terpheach?), close to which
is the high hill Cairnpaple—i.e., carn-pobull, the hill of the
people; about three miles from this is Livingstone, the Saxon
name of the MacLeas; while close to, and a little south of this, is
Bell's quarry. When were these partly Gaelic names given to
these localities?

We know that Cramond was attached to the diocese of Dunkeld,
and we have seen a Terpheach given away by grant of an Earl of
Athol, who seemed to have a right to it through the female line,
a succession quite opposed to Gaelic ideas wherever a son, even
illegitimate, was alive to head the people, and known to have been
a cause of war both in Moray and Galloway according to early
history. We have also had before us the fact that Logierait was
not long before confirmed to Scone by the Bishop of Dunkeld.
If a Gaelic tribe, with a traditional tenure of the localities men-

---

* "Proceed. Soc. Antiq., 1870," p. 272.
† "Chron. Picts and Scots," p. 12.
‡ Preface, "Chron. Picts and Scots," p. 81.

tioned, considered themselves dispossessed, the earls of Athol, the proprietor of Terpheach, and the Bishop of Dunkeld, would be the parties against whom they would have the feud. In 1407, two centuries and a-half after the grant of Terpheach and somewhat more after the confirmation of Logierait to Scone, we find Bishop Cardony of Dunkeld fleeing from his palace from marauders. Canon Mylne,* whose Latin I translate, speaking of the then bishop in the year 1441, says "he was a determined man, and conducted himself boldly against the Highlanders, holding the chief Rob Reoch MacDonoquhy as an enemy of the Church, because this chief caused the church lands of Little Dunkeld to be depopulated, which at the time were managed by a certain gentleman of the surname of Forester, and by office forester of the Torwood. And it so happened that the said Robert encountered the said Forester to the east of the Church of Auchtergavin, and suddenly attacked him, where Robert, fatally wounded in the head, did not die on the spot, but causing his head to be bound up with a linen bandage, came to the king at Perth, and procured his new feu of the lands of Strowan, in reward for his capture of the Master of Athol, and returning, after obtaining possession, died. In revenge of his death, the Clan Donoquhy, alway when called to the king's wars against the English, invade and depopulate the lands of Torwood."

This Rob Reoch, whose name is so like that of the Bodach in Mr. Campbell's "Champion," and of the saint of the Finn Faidheach, was the ancestor of the Robertsons of Strowan, in Athol, close to Logierait, which Strowan is dedicated to St. Fillan, and at which was long preserved the "Clag Buidheann," the bell of the troop.

In 1452 Bishop Lauder got the king's commission as bailie of the district, and he executed an arch robber, a certain Macbre, known as the bishop's sorner. This name seems to be a spelling of Macbeth, the same as in the Irish and Pictish additions to the Historia Britonum, where he is called Macbhretach.

But even this piece of retributive justice did not quiet Clan Donoquhy, because it appears that shortly afterwards the bishop having imprisoned one of the clan, the chief and his men marched to Dunkeld to the rescue, and finding the bishop

* "New Statistical Account," and Mylne's "Bishops of Dunkeld."

celebrating mass in the cathedral, they entered the church and let fly a shower of arrows at him, causing him to seek safety behind a beam in the choir. It seems probable that Robert Reoch, the son of Duncan above mentioned, was trying to balance old scores with all his family creditors, when he got his death at Auchtergavin.

Whether the quality of the stone of Bell's quarry is the same as that of the "Clach Mhannaidh," the Stone of Destiny (or luck),* I am not mineralogist enough to determine. I leave this for experts to settle.

Another incident in Scottish history which has given rise to a good deal of speculation, and which seems to have a connection with the Clan Donnachie, is the battle on the Inch at Perth, before Robert III., 28th September, 1396. The "Registrum Moraviense" says this combat took place because, "firma pax reformari non poterat inter duas parentelas" Clan Hay and Clan Qwhwle, "sed homicidia depredationis hinc inde committebantur cotidie "—"A firm peace could not be established between the two clans Clanhay and Clanqwhwle, but slaughters and robberies from henceforth were committed daily."

Boece calls them Irsmen (Irishmen), named Clankayis and Glenquhattanis (Clanchattans).†

The last writer on the subject, Dr. John Macpherson,‡ identifies the Clan Quhewil as a branch of the Clan Chattan, believing that the preponderance of opinion is in favour of the name Quhewil being derived from the Dougal *Phaol*,§ a marriage with whose daughter gave the chieftainship of Clanchattan to the Macintoshes, a supremacy disputed by the MacPhersons.|| Dr. Macpherson

---

* *Vide* M'Leod and Dewar's Gaelic Dictionary.

† J. H. Burton's "History of Scotland," vol. iii. p. 73; quoting from the Scotichronicon, the names of the chiefs of the two parties—"Scheabeg et suos consanguinarios qui Clankay et Cristi Johnson ac suos qui Clanquhele dicebantur. Compare with spellings of Clanquhele, "chwle" for Chumhail in Dean of Lismore, p. 68, line 9. Is not Finn mac Chumhail Finn son of the Dog of Fail, Finn mac Cu Fail, *mh* having the sound of *F*?

‡ "Proceed. Soc. Antiq.," vol. x. p. 22.

§ *Phal*, old Gaelic, for *Fail*, modern. Dean of Lismore, p. 28, line 3. Compare "quhen" (*when*), "quhilk" (*which*), "quhile" (*while*) of Bellenden, the *qu* standing for *w*; and Dean of Lismore—"waynew" for *Fhianaibh*, p. 4, last line; "in wane," *na Feinn*, p. 20, line 39; "zar weane," *de'r Feinn*, p. 24, last line; "ranyth wane," *ri na Feinn*, p. 26, line 29, &c.

|| Dr. Macpherson's Paper, p. 12.

further points out their close proximity in historical notices with the Robertsons and Macnairs, and says it is clear that the quarrel arose from the Clann Quheule having taken part in the raid on Angus in 1392, which resulted in the fight at Glascune, near Blairgowrie, at which the leaders of the Highlanders were of the Clan Donnachie.

Wyntoun in his Chronicle, however, calls the Kays by another name. He says those who fought were thirty men on each side of "Clahynnhe Qwhewyl and Clachinyhe—that is, Clanna Qwhewyl and Clachine, the Clan Qwhewyl (Mac Phaoil), and Clan Clagane (the MacClagans)." But these latter are termed Kays, &c., by other authors. Now, in the Bowhouse Book of the Black Book of Taymouth, the occupant of Clagane is called Donald Ammonach M'Keich—*i.e.*, Donald the Monk (used as a sobriquet), the son of Kay, phonetically the *a* being sounded as in *fay*, fairy, &c. Dr. Macpherson, who is entirely guiltless of these last conjectures, points out, that while at times the Keiths have been supposed to be members of the Clan Chattan confederacy, one of the Earls Marischall, in 1715, claimed kindred with some of that clan, to influence them at the time of the rebellion (*vide* MacDougall list, p. 5).

The clans who fought on the Inch are believed to have been subdivisions of the same tribe; and it may be from Dugald Phaol that the MacLagans claim their Dougal parentage. But if the Clan Quhele were MacLagans, and the Clan Clachinyhe MacClagans, the "Dubh Gall" must be sought further back; for his daughter's marriage, which carried with it a claim to represent the father, took place in 1291, according to Macpherson, and the fight at Perth was but five years more than a century later.

I am of opinion that the Clan Qwhele, put to the horn as "omnes Clan quhwil,"* after the fight at Glascune, represented the whole clan, so called, of "Cumhail," and that the clans Clachinyhe and Kay (*i.e.*, Keith or Ceith, the smith of St. Patrick, the maker of the Finn Faidheach), Clan Donnachie, Macnabs, Macnairs, &c., were, in fact, the septs into which it was divided. This, then, seems the form which the statement, that the M'lagans are a branch of the M'Clellands, took in their own country of Perthshire.

* Dr. Macpherson's Paper, p. 19.

I may mention some other possible derivations of the name Maclagan. One which I got from Mr. Thomas T. MacLagan, Classical Master at the High School of Edinburgh, and which he got from a member of the Clan M'Nab, is, "*Mac Gille Clachan Ceann;*" translated, "Son of the servant of the head man of the village." The only use of these two last words in combination that I know is *Clachan cinn*, a headstone. I never met with any designation such as that given above for a village magistrate ; and I must repudiate the idea of Maclagan meaning the son of the servant of a village potentate—possibly the son of the scavenger, if indeed such a functionary had existed in those days. Some other words suggest themselves as possible sources of derivation :—

*Lagenia*, Leinster. Mac mna Laighen, the son of the woman of Leinster, is applied to Malcolm II., son of Kenneth, in the prophecy of St. Berchan ("Chron. Picts and Scots," p. 99); and he, according to Boece, was Macbeth's as well as Duncan's maternal grandfather.

*Lagen*, a measure of ale, about a gallon or more. We have on record the number of lagens of ale to be furnished to the monks of Restennet when Alexander III. came to stay at Forfar.

*Lagan*, a hollow, said to mean a valley. M'Lagan, the son of the valley.

*Logan* or *Laggan* stones. The rocking-stones, of which one was in Kells parish, Galloway, and one in the neighbourhood of Abernethy.

*Leac Leacan*, a slab.

*Claigionn*, a skull.

*Clach*, a stone.

In the "Annals of the Four Masters," A.D. 960, the fleet of the son of Amhlaeibh, and of the *Ladgmans*, is said to have come to Ireland and plundered Conaill and Edar, with Inis Mac Neasain ; and the Ladgmans afterwards went to the men of Munster to avenge their brother (*i.e.*, Oin), so that they plundered Inis Doimhle, &c., and did much harm. In 1014, Amlain, who was killed in Dublin among others of the Gall, is called Mac Lagman. I entertain the idea that these were Gall Gael of the same tribes as those who conquered Alba with Kenneth. Lagman was a Norse title, applied to the president of a district parliament. I confess that I cannot accept any of these derivations.

I once had a conversation with a West Highland Gaelic-speaking friend as to the meaning of Maclagan. He offered at first no explanation, but subsequently suggested that MacLucas was its equivalent. It was in vain for me to try and get an explanation out of him of the reason of this; but it is noteworthy that this name is bracketed with M'Lellan in the list of MacDougalls under the head of "Mac Inishes." Is MacLucas, Mac Luigh Chas, the son of swift foot? (p. 16).

From a consideration of all that has been noted above, I am led to the opinion—

That it is possible that the first St. Fillan brought the Finn Faidheach of M'Creich from Guenedote, in Wales, through Manand (Linlithgowshire), to central Scotland;

That, after having been thrown into a pool, the Bell was recovered, and taken by its salvor, the second Fillan, to Islay;

That, carried as a palladium with its altar-stone, the La Fail, it was taken to Manand by the Scots;

That, after the defeat in Manand of the Scots by the Picts, it was taken to Ireland, where it made its appearance at O'Domhnuill's Court, in Tara, and subsequently in the northern parts of Ireland;

That, from Bangor, in Ulster, it was brought by sea to Loch Broom, and thence by land to Logierait or Scone;

That the descendants of some of those who brought it to that locality, and who believed that they could trace their descent from the Pictish-descended Welsh monarch Maelgwn, claimed a hereditary right to the Manand district, in which was the Torwood; and according to the invariable custom of naming a clan after an individual, called themselves after his name in expression of that belief;

That the writing the name Maclagan with a large L or C arose from the not unnatural supposition that Lagan or Clagan was the complete form of the name of the individual from whom the clan was named, as if it were Rob Mac Lagain or Mac Clagain—*i.e.*, Rob the son of Lagan or Clagan; whereas, as we have seen, it was written Trennecathus filius Maglagni—*i.e.*, Trennecathus mac Maglagni; *Anglice*, not Trennecathus, son of the Bell, but Trennecathus, son of the son of the Bell.

This is my theory of the etymology of the Clan Maclagan.

# LIST OF WORKS REFERRED TO.

An Irish-English Dictionary, by Edward O'Reilly. With a Supplement, by John O'Donovan, LL.D., M.R.I.A. Dublin, 1877.

A Dictionary of the Gaelic Language, by the Rev. Dr. Norman M'Leod, and the Rev. Dr. Daniel Dewar. Glasgow and London, 1866.

Sculptured Stones of Scotland. Printed for the Spalding Club. Edited by John Stuart. Aberdeen, 1856.

Vitæ Dunkeldensis Ecclesiæ Episcoporum, A.D. 1515. Ab Alexandro Myln, ejusdem ecclesiæ canonico conscriptæ. Edinburgh, 1823.

Fasti Ecclesiæ Scoticanæ : The Succession of Ministers in the Parish Churches of Scotland, from 1860 to the present time, by Hew Scott, A.M. Edinburgh, 1866.

The Black Book of Taymouth, with other papers from the Breadalbane Charter Room. Edinburgh, 1855.

Caledonia ; or, An Account, Historical and Topographic, of North Britain, from the most ancient to the present times ; with a Dictionary of Places, Chorographical and Philological, by George Chalmers, F.R.S. and S.A. London, 1807.

History and Chronicles of Scotland, written in Latin by Hector Boece, Canon of Aberdeen, and translated by John Bellenden, Archdeacon of Moray and Canon of Ross. Edinburgh, 1831.

Annals of the Kingdom of Ireland, by the Four Masters, from the earliest period to the year 1616. By John O'Donovan, LL.D., M.R.I.A. Second Edition, 1856.

Lectures on the Manuscript Materials of Ancient Irish History, by Eugene O'Curry. Re-issue, 1878.

Kalendars of Scottish Saints, by Alex. Penrose Forbes, D.C.L., Bishop of Brechin. 1872.

Transactions Royal Irish Academy.

Celtic Scotland : A History of Ancient Alban, by William F. Skene. Vols. I. and II. 1876.

Proceedings of the Society of Antiquaries of Scotland.

The Coronation Stone, by William F. Skene. 1869.

The New Statistical Account of Scotland, by the Ministers of the respective Parishes. 1845.

Life of St. Columba, Founder of Hy, written by Adamnan, ninth Abbot of that Monastery. By William Reeves, D.D., M.R.I.A. Edinburgh, 1874.

The Martyrology of Donegal : A Calendar of the Saints of Ireland, translated by John O'Donovan, LL.D. Edited by J. H. Todd, D.D., and William Reeves, D.D. Dublin, 1864.

The Ecclesiastical Architecture of Ireland, anterior to the Anglo-Norman Invasion, comprising an Essay on the Origin and Uses of the Round Towers of Ireland, by George Petrie, R.H.A. Second Edition, 1845.

Popular Tales of the West Highlands, orally collected, with a Translation by J. F. Campbell. Edinburgh, 1860.

The Dean of Lismore's Book : A Selection of Ancient Gaelic Poetry, from a Manuscript Collection, made by Sir James M'Gregor, Dean of Lismore, in the beginning of the sixteenth century. By the Rev. Thomas M'Lauchlan. Introduction and additional notes, by W. F. Skene. Edinburgh, 1862.

Lectures on Welsh Philology, by John Rhys, M.A. London, 1877.

Britain ; or, A Chorographical Description of the most flourishing Kingdoms of England, Scotland, Ireland, &c., written in Latin by William Camden, translated into English by Philemon Holland, M.D. London, 1637.

The Gael. An Gaidheal ; paipeir-naidheachd agus leabhair-sgeoil gaidhealach. Edinburgh, 1872-77.

LORIMER AND GILLIES, PRINTERS, 31 ST. ANDREW SQUARE, EDINBURGH.

www.ingramcontent.com/pod-product-compliance
Lightning Source LLC
Chambersburg PA
CBHW020818030726
47496CB00009B/2937